MW01243502

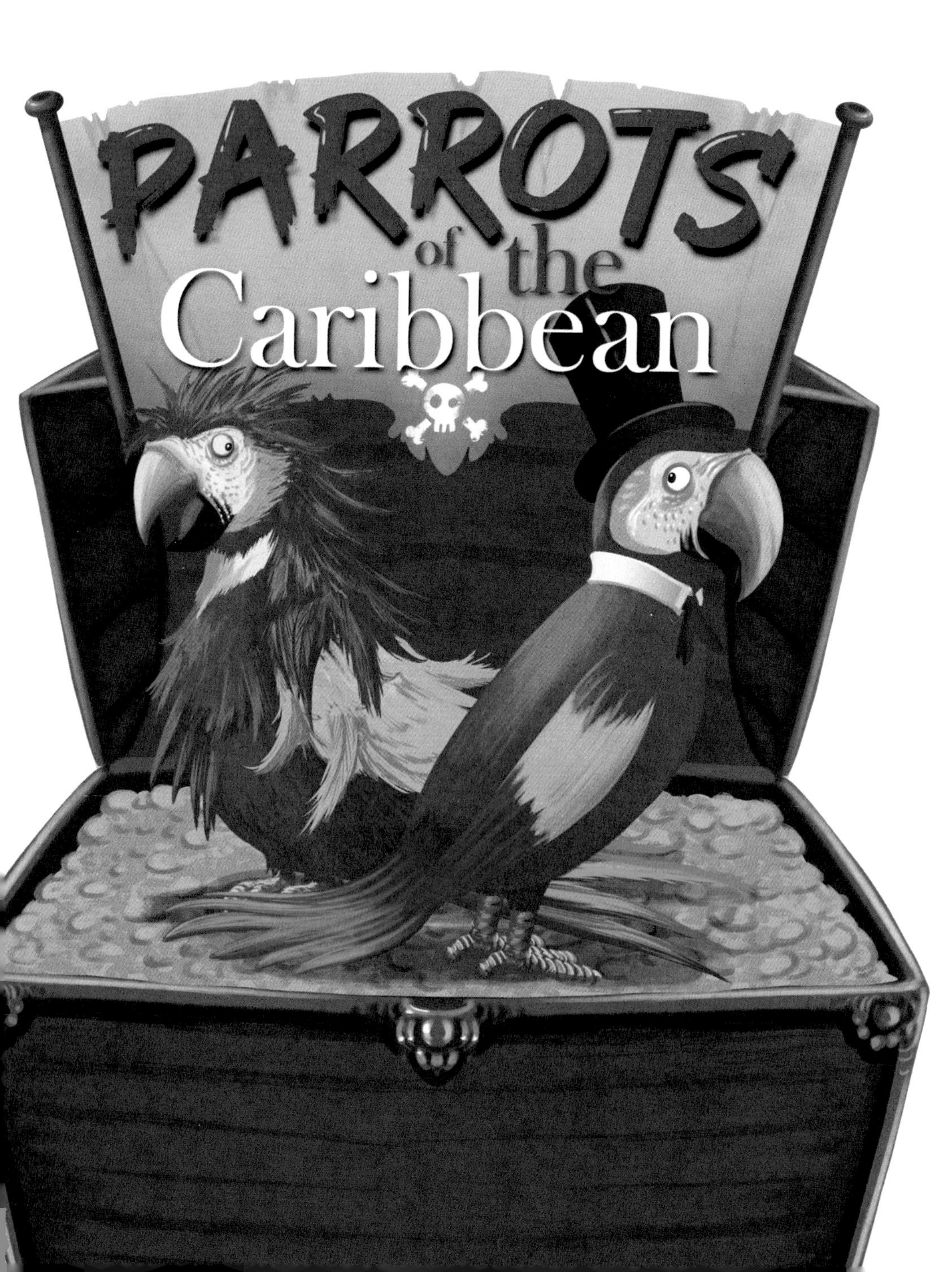
PARROTS'
of the
Caribbean

About the authors

The authors are a daughter who grew up convinced that her father's ancestors were probably pirates, and a father who allowed the illusion to thrive, and helped her pass it along to the grandchildren.

Rachel Shifra Tal and Edward Truitt

Illustrations by Leonardo Ariel Ariza Ardila.

Dedicated to pirates everywhere, and the parrots that put up with them.

Rumball was a disgrace to all parrot kind! His feathers stuck out at all angles and he smelled indescribably bad, even for a pirate's parrot. His pet pirate was Captain Redbeard. Redbeard smelled worse than month-old socks and wet dog, and he had the dirtiest ship afloat; it was filthy even by pirate standards, and that is really dirty! The crew never did mind for they smelled even worse!

They were the stinkiest pirates ever, for you could smell them coming from miles away!

Captain Redbeard kept a most untidy ship and usually lost most his treasure before he could bury it. Captain Redbeard's ship was a floating wreck, and the crew would often fall over the unusually large supply of empty rum bottles rolling from side to side.

The maps were all greasy, the compass was bent, the wheel was missing half its spokes and the sails were more hole than sail. It was a slow ship, too slow to catch many trade ships. It was so slow and the crew was so drunk that once, when they ran aground on a sand bar, it was two days before anyone noticed that they were not getting anywhere. It is a wonder they had any treasure at all, but people would pay them just to go away whenever they came to plunder.

Then there were the fleas, they got so bad that even the bilge rats jumped ship. They all went ashore at the Tortugas and got jobs as pub rats.

The food was so bad that most of the sailors drank rum instead. Rumball too. He was a particularly pickled pirate's parrot. That explains all the empty rum bottles rolling about. But it doesn't make for a very happy crew.

Whenever they went ashore they ate a lot of junk food, drank more rum, and stuffed themselves so much that the ship was hours late getting out of port again. However, this was not a problem because the Royal Navy didn't bother chasing them. They were far too dirty for jail, and the townspeople would always pay Redbeard's crew to leave, but only after the pirates spent all their money on junk food and rum.

At the far end of the Caribbean, Montague was a very posh parrot. He lived with another pirate who was also named Redbeard. Montague had not one feather out of place and even wore a top hat.

You could never mix up Montague's Captain Redbeard with that Other Redbeard! He was way too neat for a pirate. He polished the gangplank twice a day. Montague would even hold a mirror for his Captain as they pirated to check his reflection for flaws. He kept his crew to the same standard of polish as his shiny deck.

There were no rats on this pirate ship, for the cook kept such a spotless galley that they could find nothing to eat. A pirate ship without rats, really is no pirate ship at all.

However, it was a wonder that they ever got any treasure either. You see, this Redbeard did not like to fire his cannons because they got all dirty. After a while, all the treasure ships knew, and they would just wave politely and keep on sailing. This disappointed the crew, but no bad language was allowed. And pirates get a little frustrated when they can't cuss and swear. It's half the fun of being a pirate.

As for rum, that was too low class for Captain Redbeard. He served white wine and little drinks with umbrellas in them every afternoon precisely at 5.

When Captain Redbeard was ironing a pirate flag one sunny morning, Montague, who was watching to make sure he did it right, noticed some faint writing on the back. He hopped down from Redbeard's shoulder for a closer look, nearly getting his feathers singed by the hot iron. He was delighted to find that it was half of a treasure map! After much squawking and flapping, Captain Redbeard noticed it too.

Being a pirate, although a very neat one, he realized that treasure was treasure and a buried treasure was the best kind, for he did not have to dirty his cannons to get it. Captain Redbeard ordered his crew to set sail on the course to a secret destination known only to him and Montague.

Montague was very discrete. He considered himself above talking with any common pirates, and on occasion was a bit snobbish about Redbeard himself.

Meanwhile, the other Redbeard (the dirty one) always flew a skull and crossbones with only one bone. But one day, while pillaging, Redbeard found a new flag with both bones. However, being a slovenly pirate, he never threw anything away, so he tossed the one-boned flag into a moldering pile of rum bottles. While rummaging for his cutlass one day, he stopped to wipe his brow with the first thing that came to hand, which just happened to be his old skull and crossbone. Rumball, who was perched on his shoulder, noticed to his greed and excitement, that a treasure map was written under the skull. He nipped him on the ear and hopped up and down until Captain Redbeard finally noticed the map. It was not until they set sail and were halfway to the treasure, that they realized that they had but half the map. Arrggh.

Rumball and Redbeard reached the treasure island first, even though his ship was extremely slow, Redbeard reached the treasure island first because he did not have very far to go. This was good, because Redbeard's navigation was not so great. And, since he had a map of only the western half of the island, he landed in a cove on the west side. Telling the crew that he was going to go dig for clams, he took a shovel and his half of the map and set off in search of the buried treasure. Rumball stayed aboard because he had an exceptionally bad rumover after celebrating their arrival.

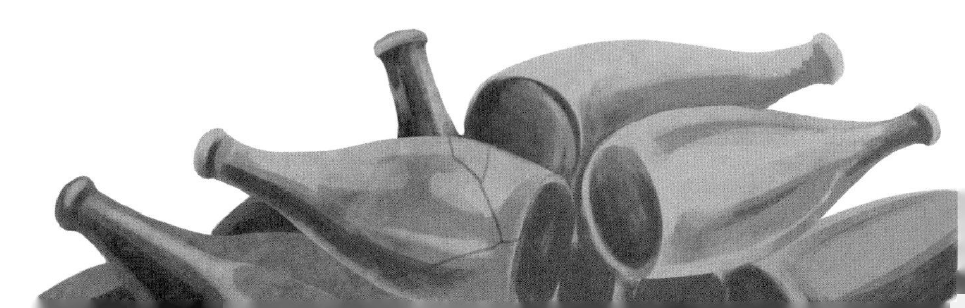

Following a stream clearly marked on his map (not even Redbeard could miss it), he soon came to a waterfall, with a cave marked on the map behind it. The smudged half of an "X" marking the treasure looked like it was just a little way into the cave. Redbeard hated getting wet, which is an awkward problem for a sailor, and he looked for a way around the waterfall to get into the cave.

There was no other way. Putting the shovel over his head to keep his pirate hat dry, he made his way through the waterfall, getting a halfway decent shower in the process. He was a bit cleaner by the time he got into the cave, although he smelled like wet pirate, and that smells even worse than a dry pirate. However, he slipped on a wet rock and bonked his head, knocking himself completely out.

Meanwhile, Montague and his Redbeard had docked that very same day on the east side of the Island. Montague didn't like going ashore because the shore parrots always made fun of his top hat.

Soon, the clean Redbeard was steadily making his orderly way to the cave as well. He and Montague did not tell the crew where he was going either. He took a lamp and his map and his 'going ashore for treasure' kit. However he decided not to take a shovel because digging would get his boots dirty, not to mention the shovel.

Deep in the cave, a very wet Redbeard woke up a while later with a headache worse than his last rumover. He staggered upright and felt for his shovel and his hand happened upon a rusty chest instead. Shovel forgotten, he felt his way out of the cave with the heavy chest tucked under his arml but he went out the easterly side by mistake and followed the neat set of footprints right back to the other cove.

There was something strange about the pirate ship anchored in the cove, but he was much too busy trying to sneak his treasure aboard without being seen to notice what exactly was different. Climbing in through his cabin window and heaving the rusty chest aboard, the dirty and wet Redbeard was shocked to see a parrot in a top hat! The parrot (who was actually Montague) was even more surprised to see a wet dirty mess of a pirate climbing through HIS cabin window! This horrible smelling pirate had a red beard but was definitely not the red-bearded pirate he knew!

The dirty pirate hardly noticed the cleanliness of his ship and crew, in fact he never did notice that it was not even his ship! He ordered rum for all to celebrate his treasure! The crew having never been allowed such a party before, were soon as dirty as pirates should be and never noticed anything amiss with their captain. Since the captain never told them to clean up, the ship quickly became a floating dump. Everyone was happy with the new state of affairs, except for Montague.

He hated the taste of rum and couldn't tolerate the smell aboard. He was one very unhappy parrot.

Meanwhile the neat Captain Redbeard found the cave with no trouble and stepped through the waterfall with his trusty parasol that he brought to protect his complexion from the sun; red-bearded pirates tended to burn in the tropical sun. Lighting his lantern and holding his nose because of the strange smell the cave seemed to have, Redbeard to his delight, soon found a shiny gold chest that had the satisfying clink of treasure when he rattled it.

Holding his nose, parasol, treasure, lantern, and his map was proving quite difficult. He slipped down a wet rock into a puddle of mud, putting out his lantern in the process. Sitting up in a slimy, cold, wet, stinky puddle in the dark, Redbeard thought this must be the worst day of his life.

Then he remembered the treasure.

Groping around in the slime, he found his now-dirty chest and struggled to his feet. The lantern was too wet to light, so he had to feel his way out of the cave. Fortunately, he could hear the waterfall, and soon saw daylight ahead. He was so happy to find his way out, that for once in his life, he didn't mind getting soaking wet.

In his haste to get back to his clean clothes and a bath, he didn't notice that the footprints he was following back to his ship were heading in the wrong direction.

When he got to the cove, he stopped in horror almost dropping the treasure at the scene in front of him!

How long had he been gone?

His ship was in absolute shambles! Storming aboard, he was horrified to see the state of Montague (actually Rumball), who was drunk, and dishevelled, with his feathers sticking out at odd angles. The smell of ship and the state of the crew was indescribable. Scooping up the bird with his handkerchief, he ordered all his crew to take a bath as well.

The crew, never having been ordered to bathe in their lives, barely knew how to go about it. But Montague (Rumball) had the worst time of all. He sobered up right quick during a vigorous scrubbing and was beginning to wonder what was wrong with the captain. It took Rumball longer than most parrots to figure things out.

Other than their bath, the crew were happy to discover that their captain had a change of heart when they put into the nearest port. The captain spent the treasure on new clothes for everyone and a top hat for Rumball.

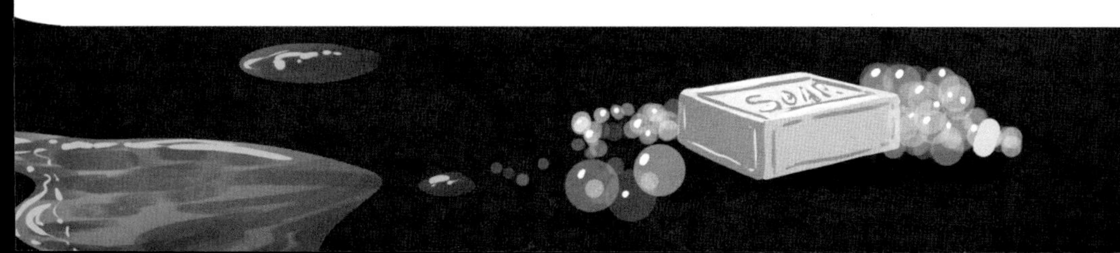

He also hired a decent cook. Despite buying the finest feather conditioner to be found in the Caribbean, one or two of his feathers never quite looked right. The now well-dressed, spot-less crew was happy to discover their love of white wine and healthy finger food, not to mention the umbrellas in the drinks.

Rumball hated being called Montague but he hated white wine even more. He was a most unhappy parrot.

One fine day, the two ships happened to pass each other on the open sea. Neither captain nor crew noticed the other ship, but the two unhappy birds did!

Neither captain or crew noticed his old ship sailing by, but the two unhappy birds did! They each flew back to be with their rightful Redbeard.

Made in the USA
Middletown, DE
08 October 2023